The
Christmas Carol

retold by Mark A. Taylor
illustrated by Jim Talbot

Ebenezer Scrooge was frowning.

Christmas carolers on the corner sang a cheery tune. But Scrooge didn't listen.

Red bows and pine branches decorated every shop window. But Scrooge didn't care.

"Christmas is for simpletons to waste their money," he grumbled, as he came to his office. "My partner, Jacob Marley, understood that. But he's been dead for seven long years!"

He opened the door and said out loud, "You won't catch me frittering away a fortune on one stupid day!"

The office was cold and dark.

"Good morning, Mr. Scrooge," squeaked Bob Cratchit, a thin-faced young man at a desk in the far corner.

"Merry Christmas, Uncle Scrooge," said his smiling nephew, Fred, from the center of the room.

"Bah, humbug!" growled Scrooge. "What are YOU doing here?" he snarled at Fred.

"I've come to invite you to our Christmas dinner tomorrow," Fred answered, as he patted his uncle on the arm.

"I won't be there," said Scrooge. "Christmas is a day just like any other, and we'll be working."

Cratchit's eyes fell to his desk as Fred put his arm around Scrooge's shoulder. "Nonsense!" he said brightly. "We'll be looking for you, Uncle Ebenezer! Everyone needs his family at Christmas!"

As Fred left, Scrooge went to his desk, where he spent the rest of the day counting his money. Long after dark, he looked up at Cratchit. "I suppose you want to go home now," he complained.

"Sir, about tomorrow—"

"Oh, stay home if you must," Scrooge growled. "But be back before dawn the next day, to make up for the time off."

Cratchit grabbed his hat and bounded for the door. "Oh, thank you, Mr. Scrooge! Thank you very much!"

Scrooge was still frowning as he walked the cold, shadowy streets toward his home. "Cratchit needs to be more like Jacob Marley," he muttered. He raised his collar against the wind. "Marley kept his money for himself, instead of giving it to others to waste."

As he walked up his wide front steps, Scrooge reached for the handle, glanced up at the door, and gasped. The familiar lion-head door knocker was now the exact image of Jacob Marley!

Scrooge trembled as he yanked open the door and rushed into the
house. He locked the door behind him and raced up the long, dark
stairway to his bedroom.

He fumbled with a match, trying to light the lamp in his room.
And then he heard the sound of heavy chains, clanking, clanking,
clanking—past the front door, up the stairs, outside his room.

"Who's there?" said Scrooge. He backed up until he tripped and
fell into his bed. The chains came right through the wall, wrapped
around a gray ghost whose chalky face looked just like the knocker on
Scrooge's door!

"Marley!" Scrooge gasped.

"Yes, Ebenezer, it is I," the ghost of Jacob Marley said. "I have
come to warn you, Ebenezer. You need not live—or die—as selfishly as
did!"

Scrooge shivered in a corner of his bed.

"You must listen to every spirit you will meet tonight," said
Marley. "The Ghost of Christmas Past. The Ghost of Christmas Presen
The Ghost of Christmas Future. You can escape my fate!"

Marley disappeared, and Scrooge went to sleep on top of his bed.

Scrooge awoke with a start and looked around his room. He heard nothing except the low, sad toll of one a.m. from the town's clock tower.

Suddenly a strange figure stood by his bed. He shielded his eyes against the bright light coming from the crown on its head. "I am the Ghost of Christmas Past," the crowned spirit said.

"Wh-whose past?" Scrooge asked.

"Come with me, and you shall see," the ghost replied. He moved to the window ledge beside Scrooge's bed.

Scrooge reached out, the ghost took his hand, and they began to glide through the sky. Soon they came to rest beside a brightly lit window. They heard music and laughter on the other side.

"Look," the ghost said to Scrooge, and suddenly they were inside, at the edge of a lively Christmas party.

The ghost pointed at a young man dancing with a beautiful woman in the center of the room.

"That's me!" Scrooge said. "And the lovely girl—I remember her!"

"And do you remember this?" the ghost asked as he whisked Scrooge away. Now they stood in a corner of Scrooge's office. Scrooge, a few years older, sat at his desk, while the same young woman stood beside him.

"You'll never change," she whimpered, as a tear trickled down her pink cheek. "You say you love me, but all you care about is your money." She marched toward the door and then looked back at the young Scrooge. "I hope your money makes you happy," she said. "Because you'll have to enjoy it without me!"

"No, no!" Scrooge wailed, as the ghost lifted him away from the office. "Let me talk to her. I never should have let her go!"

Now Scrooge was tossing and turning in his bed. "I'm sorry, I'm sorry, I'm sorry . . ." He sat straight up, rubbed his eyes, and looked across the room. A giant, dressed in a green velvet robe and sitting on beautiful throne, smiled at him from a lavish banquet table.

Scrooge stood and saw mountains of food. "What is all this?" He walked to the giant. "Who are you?"

"You know," the giant answered as he took a bite from a large re apple.

Scrooge began to back away from him. "You are another ghost—'

"The Ghost of Christmas Present," he said. He touched Scrooge's shoulder, and at once they were on a narrow street crowded with tiny, tumble-down houses.

"This is a terrible neighborhood," said Scrooge. "Get me out of
here!"

"In time," answered the ghost. He led Scrooge to the small window
of the house closest to them. "First look inside."

Scrooge peered through the thick glass and saw Bob Cratchit at a
simple table with five children. His wife stirred an iron pot hanging in
the stone fireplace. Another child, younger and smaller than the rest,
hobbled toward the table on crutches.

"What are we having for our Christmas dinner?" the small boy asked.

"Oh, Tiny Tim, it will be a marvelous meal!" Cratchit said to his crippled son.

"Yes, we have meat in our broth tonight," said Cratchit's wife as she spooned steaming liquid from the pot into bowls. "And after dinner, one piece of bright, red hard candy for each of you!"

Cratchit smiled at his family. "We should all be grateful to Mr. Scrooge for letting me spend the whole holiday at home with you," he said.

"Grateful!" shouted Mrs. Cratchit, her eyes narrow and her mouth turned down. "That selfish monster treats you like a slave, and pays you almost nothing! *I* would be grateful if I could give him a piece of my mind!"

Scrooge backed away from the window. "She hates me," he whispered. "They—they don't have enough to eat! And the littlest one . . . he needs to see a doctor!" he said and turned toward the ghost behind him.

But no one was there.

Just then an icy wind whooshed around Scrooge, chilling him through his thin nightshirt.

Scrooge peered into the darkness and watched a shadowy phantom approach. Only a pointy white finger and two glowing eyes were visible beneath the hooded black robe it wore.

"Wh—what do you w—w—want?" Scrooge was shaking from head to heel.

The spirit was silent. The phantom turned his back to Scrooge and motioned for Scrooge to follow. Scrooge floated after him.

They stopped at a rusting, iron fence.

"The cemetery!" Scrooge murmured. "Oh, no—*why* the cemetery?"

Still the spirit refused to speak, but he led Scrooge beyond the cemetery gate to the graves. The bony finger pointed to one headstone.

Scrooge felt a hard, hot lump in his throat as he bent down in front of the marker and pulled weeds away from it. He read the inscription: EBENEZER SCROOGE

"No!" Scrooge gasped. "It can't end like this!" He stood and shouted, "I'll change! I'll change!"

Scrooge awoke in a heap of covers on his bed as the clock tower tolled eight. He jumped to his feet and threw open the window. "Hey, there!" he called to a young boy walking on the street below. "What day is it?"

"Why, it's Christmas, of course!" he said.

"Good!" said Scrooge. "I'm not too late!" He rushed down his stairs and out the door. "I'll give you a silver coin if you'll do me an errand," he said, and the boy gladly agreed. Scrooge sent him to buy a giant turkey and told him to deliver it to the home of Bob Cratchit.

"Don't tell him who sent it," Scrooge whispered in the lad's ear. "He must never know."

Scrooge spent the rest of Christmas day at his nephew's home, laughing, eating, and enjoying himself. He stayed at Fred's party until late into the evening, yet he still managed to get to work early the next day. But Bob Cratchit was not early to work. In fact, he didn't arrive until twenty minutes past nine! Scrooge looked forward to catching Bob in his tardiness.

"You're late!" said Scrooge with a frown. "Never again, Cratchit," he said. And then he smiled. "Never again will you have to worry about feeding your family or making sure Tiny Tim can see a doctor. I'm giving you a raise!"

And so he did. Not only did Scrooge increase Cratchit's salary, but he also took care of Tim's needs and those of many others in the city. His newfound joy and generosity were noticed by all who met him.

"God bless you, Mr. Scrooge," said Tim in his small voice. "God bless us every one!"